Hallelujah!

a christmas celebration

by W. Nikola-Lisa • paintings by Synthia Saint James

ATHENEUM BOOKS FOR YOUNG READERS
NEW YORK LONDON TORONTO SYDNEY SINGAPORE

To Gabriella—
may your life be filled with mystery
W. N.-L.

For the joy within us all
S. S. J.

Atheneum Books for Young Readers
An imprint of Simon & Schuster
Children's Publishing Division
1230 Avenue of the Americas
New York, New York 10020

Text copyright © 2000
by W. Nikola-Lisa
Paintings copyright © 2000
by Synthia Saint James

Book design by Ann Bobco
The text of this book is set in Mrs. Eaves.

10 9 8 7 6 5 4 3 2 1
Library of Congress Cataloging-in-
Publication Data
Nikola-Lisa, W.
Hallelujah! : a Christmas celebration /
by W. Nikola-Lisa ; illustrated by Synthia
Saint James.—1st ed.
p. cm.
Summary: Describes the plum-purple
sky, yew-green hills, silver strands of
moonlight, and other colorful things
which provide the setting for the birth of
a black baby Jesus.
ISBN 10: 1-4424-0224-5
ISBN 13: 978-1-4424-0224-9
1. Jesus Christ—Nativity—
Juvenile fiction.
[1. Jesus Christ—Nativity—Fiction.
2. Blacks—Fiction.
3. Christmas—Fiction.
4. Color—Fiction.]
I. Saint James, Synthia, ill. II. Title.
PZ7.N5855Hal 1999 [E]—dc21
97-49121 CIP AC

FIRST
EDITION

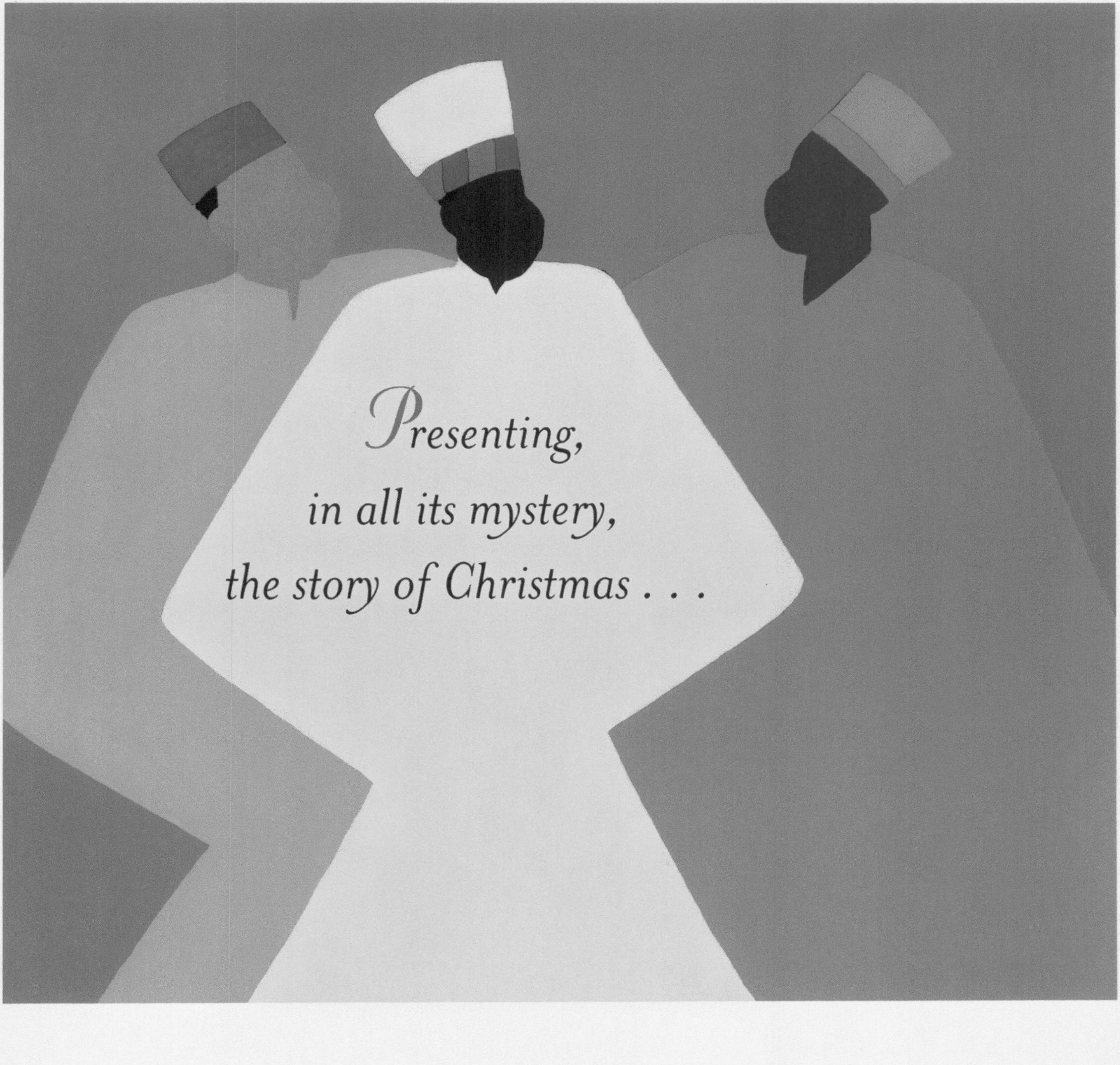

Presenting,
in all its mystery,
the story of Christmas . . .

A sprinkle of stars,

A plume of smoke,

A plum-purple sky,

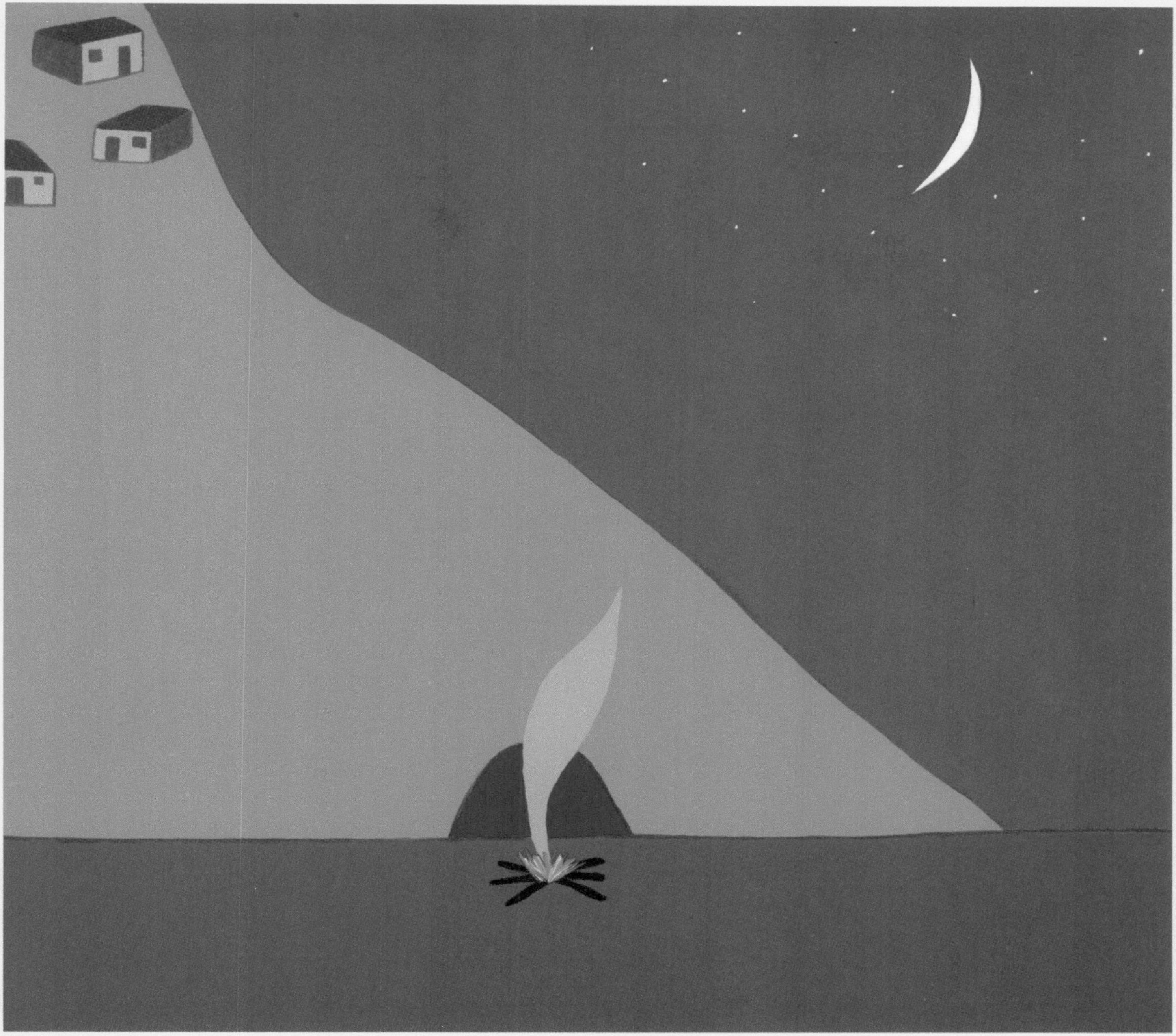

And a black baby Jesus—

Hallelujah!

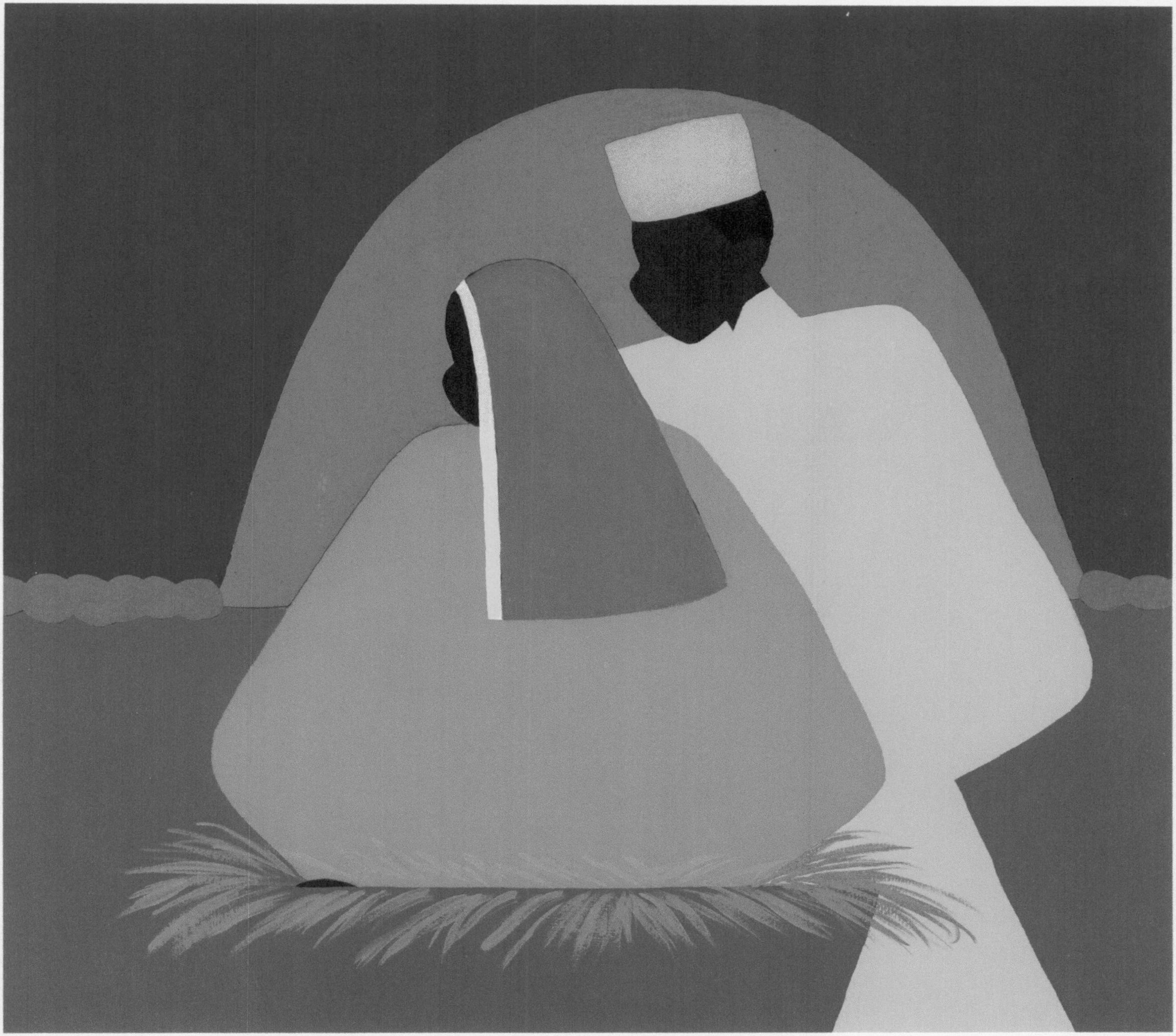

A flock of sheep,

A watch of shepherds,

Yew-green hills,

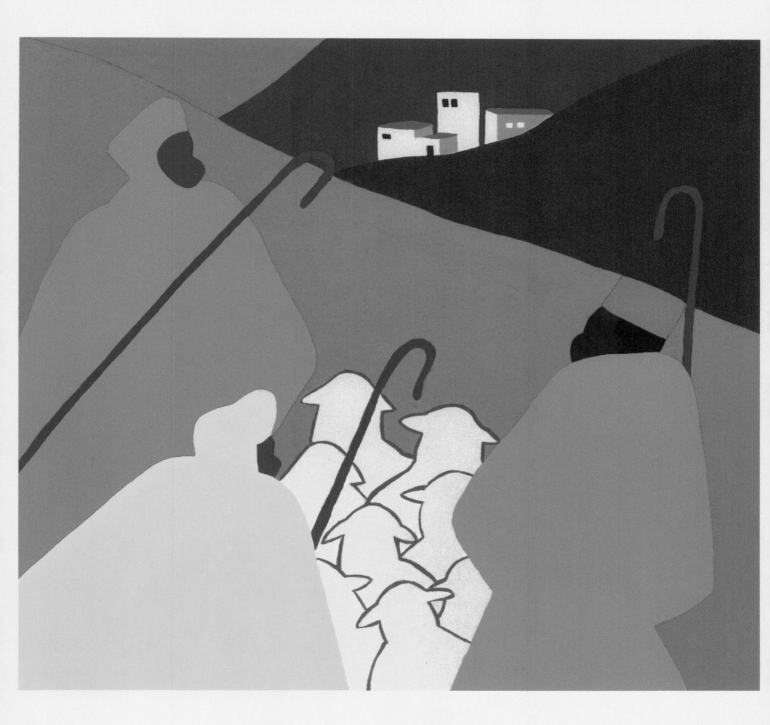

And a black baby Jesus—

Hallelujah!

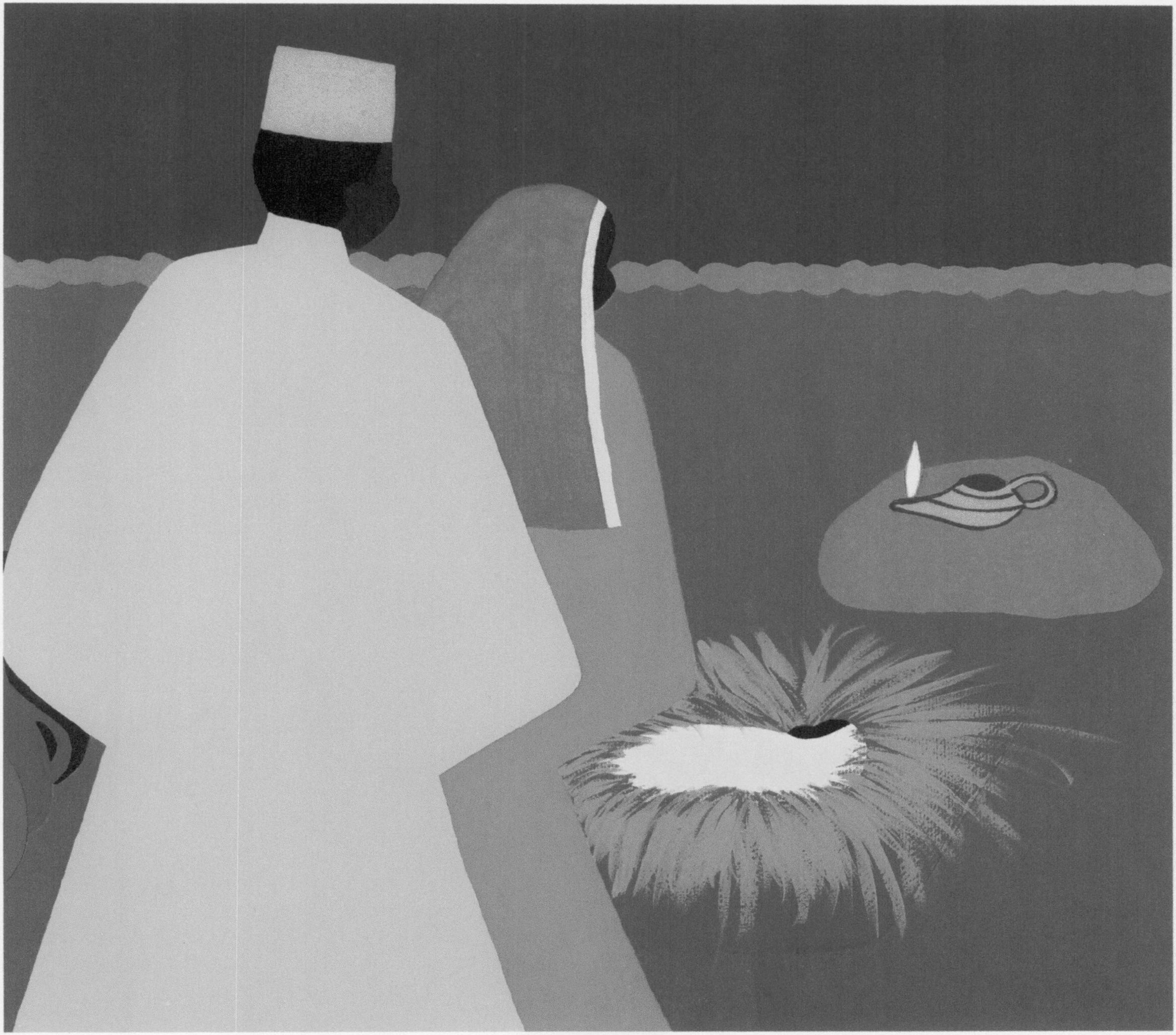

A slice of road,

A clutch of trees,

A cake-white wall,

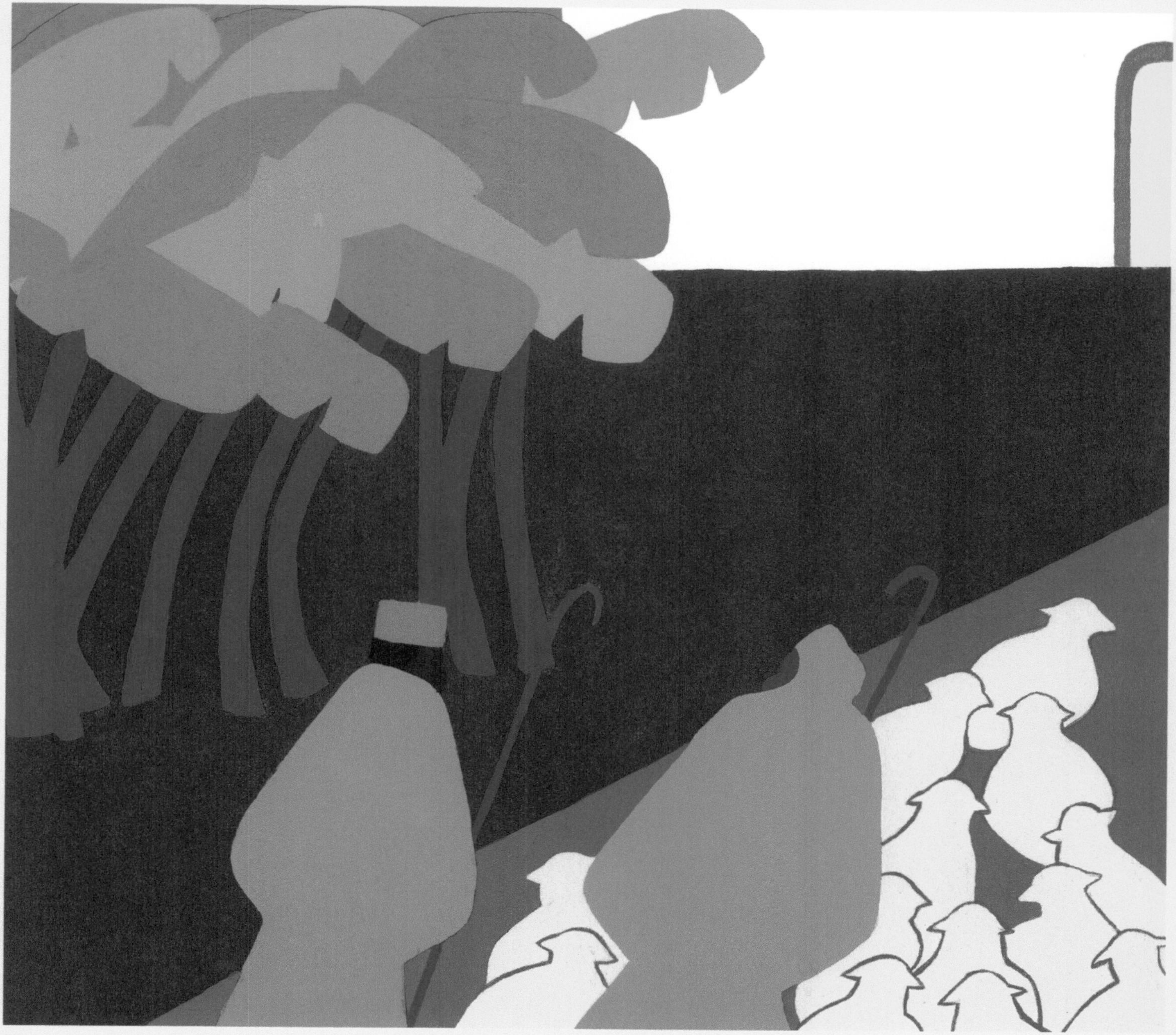

And a black baby Jesus—

Hallelujah!

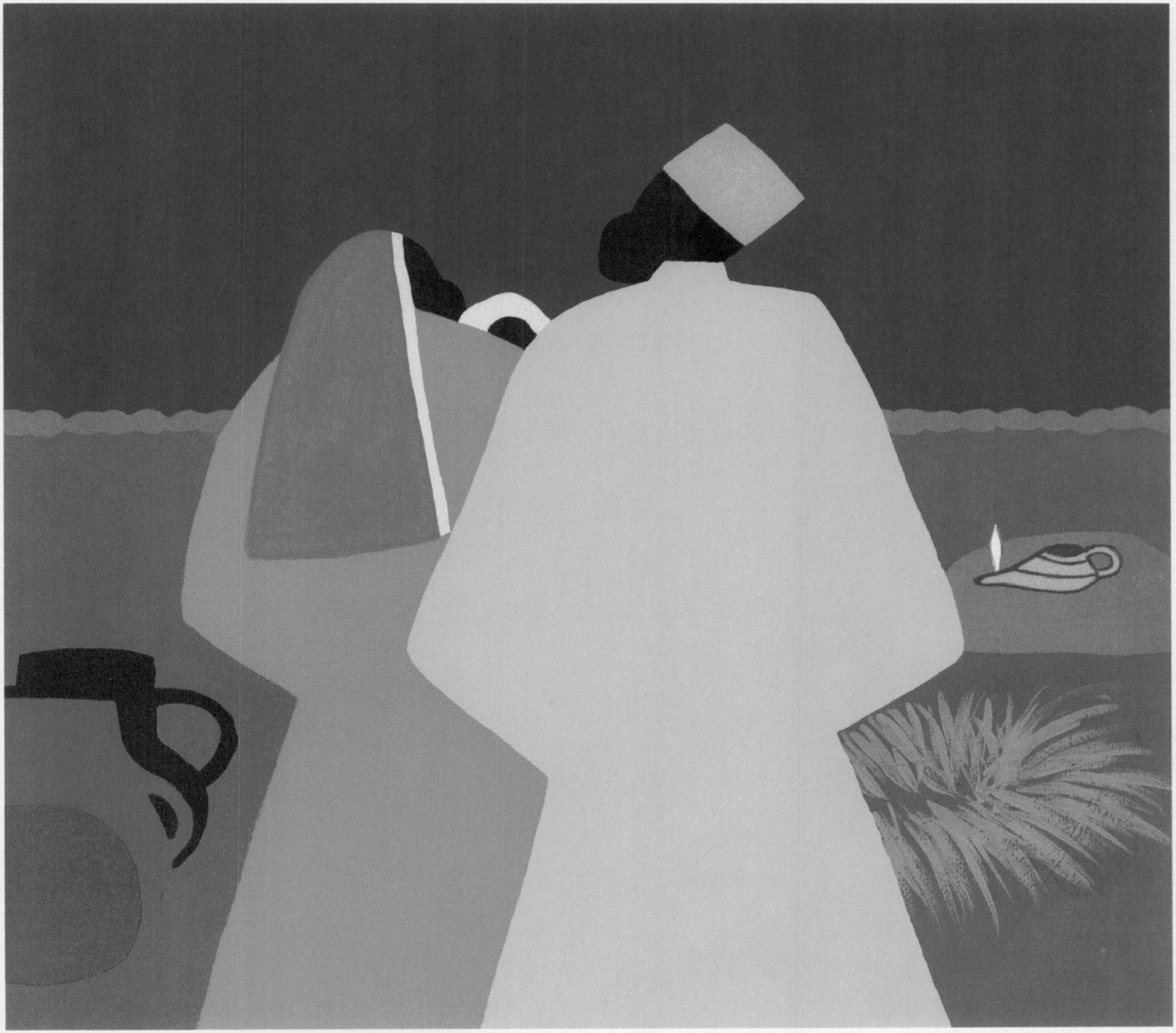

A toss of hay,

A fold of blanket,

A sky-blue scarf,

And a black baby Jesus—

Hallelujah!

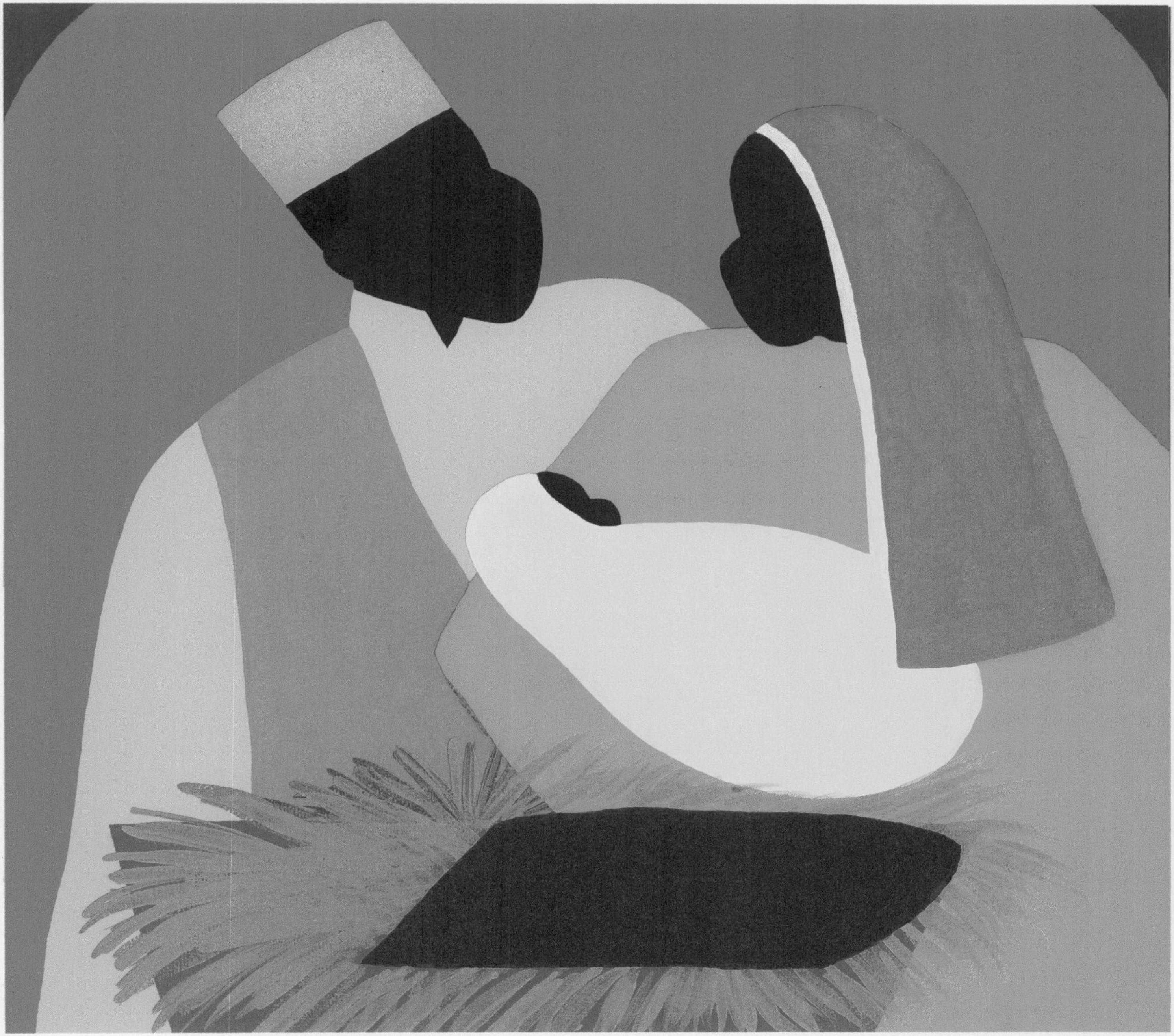

A shadowed wall,

A rumpled coat,

A slate-gray donkey,

And a black baby Jesus—

Hallelujah!

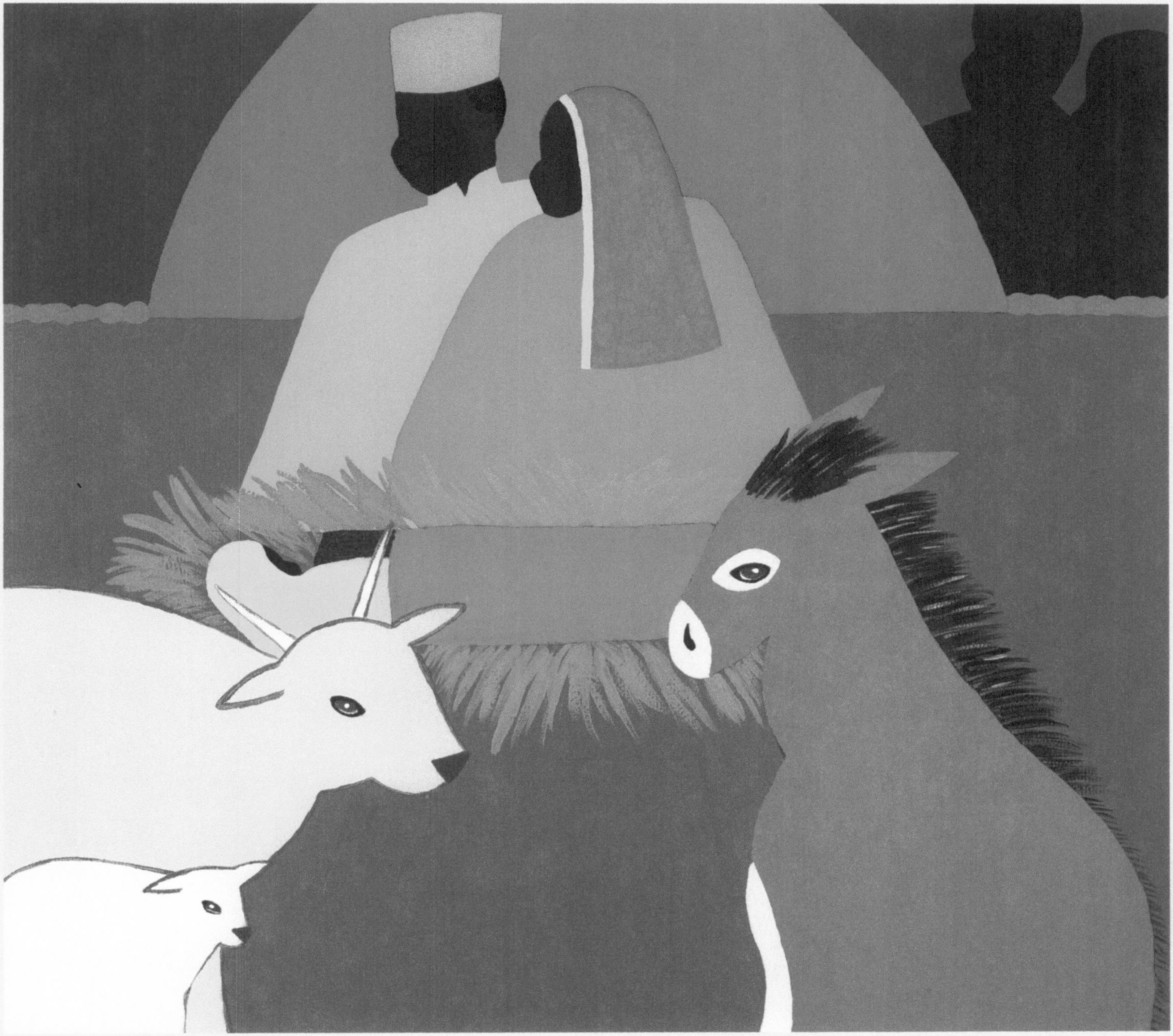

A host of angels,

A warmth of doves,

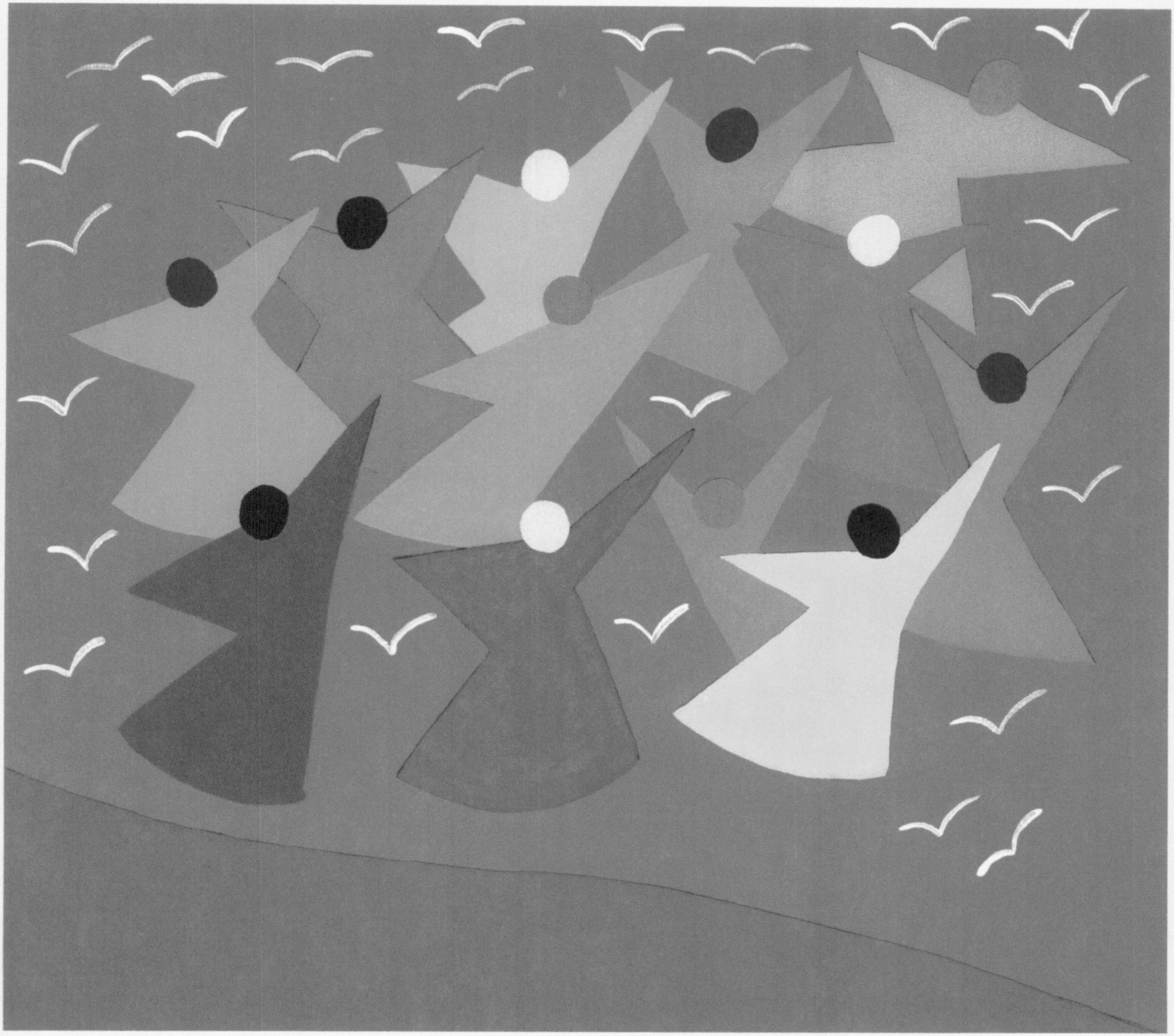

Silver strands of moonlight,
And a black baby Jesus—

Hallelujah!

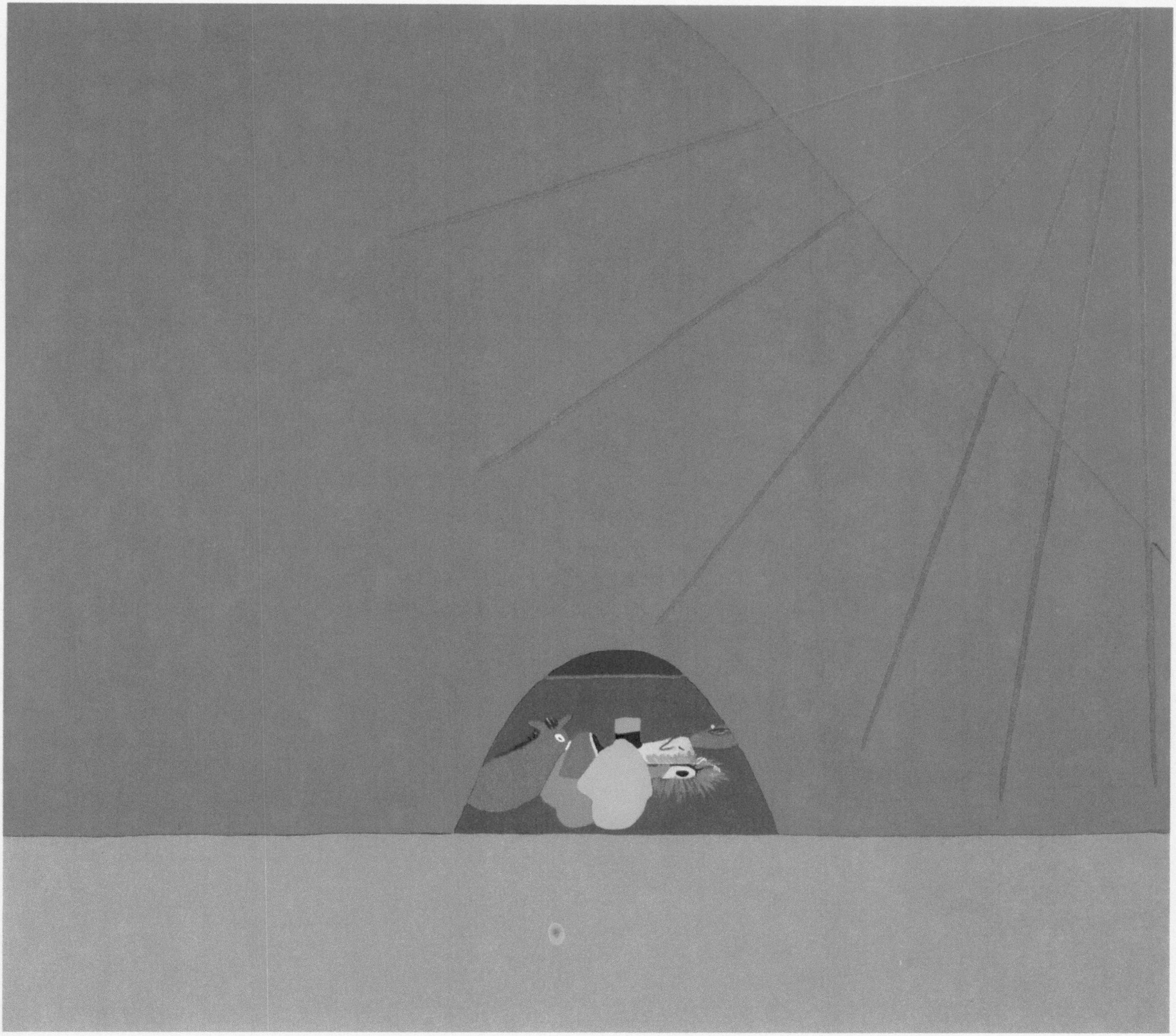

A royal crown,

A jewel-studded vest,

A red velvet canopy,

And a black baby Jesus—

Hallelujah!

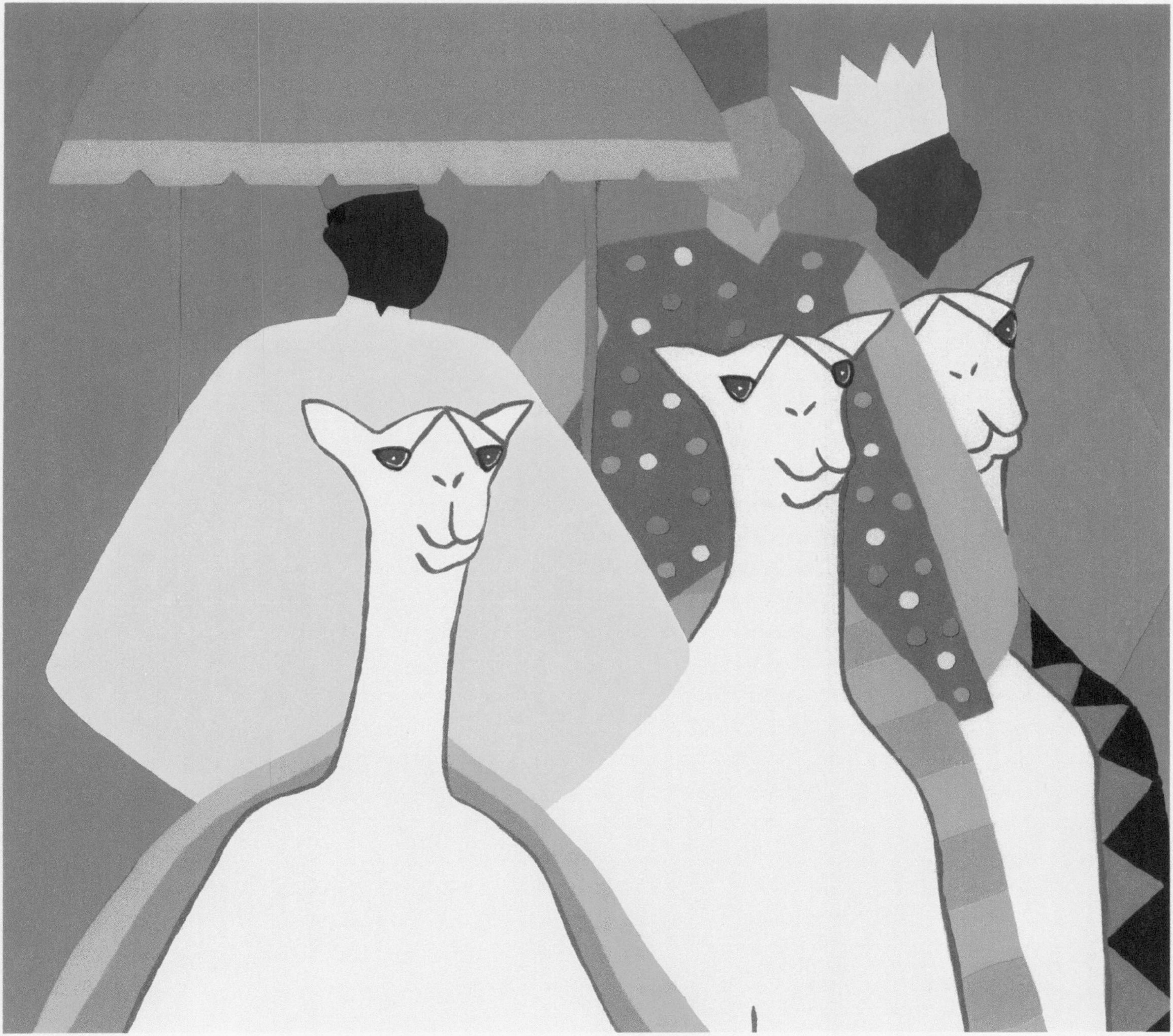

A handful of rubies,

An armful of silk,

A solid gold ring,

And a black baby Jesus—

Hallelujah!

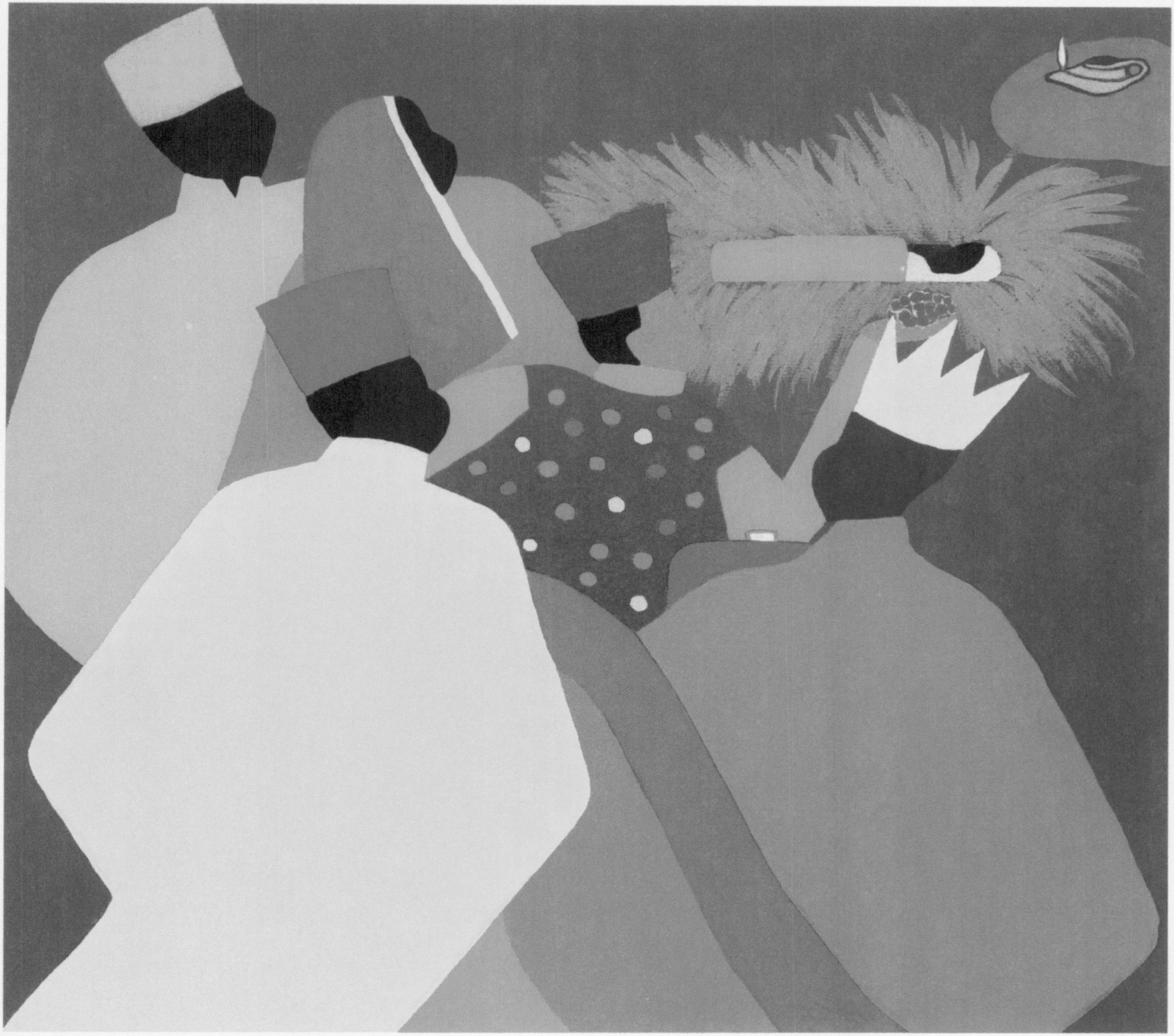

A father's smile,

A mother's touch,

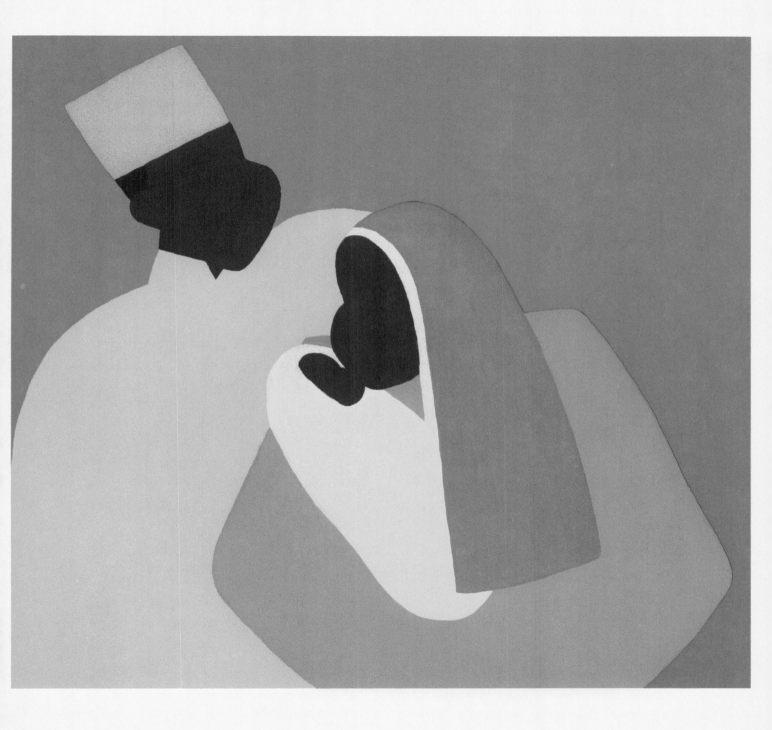

And the aura of splendor
Around a black baby Jesus—

Hallelujah!

Hallelujah!

Hallelujah!

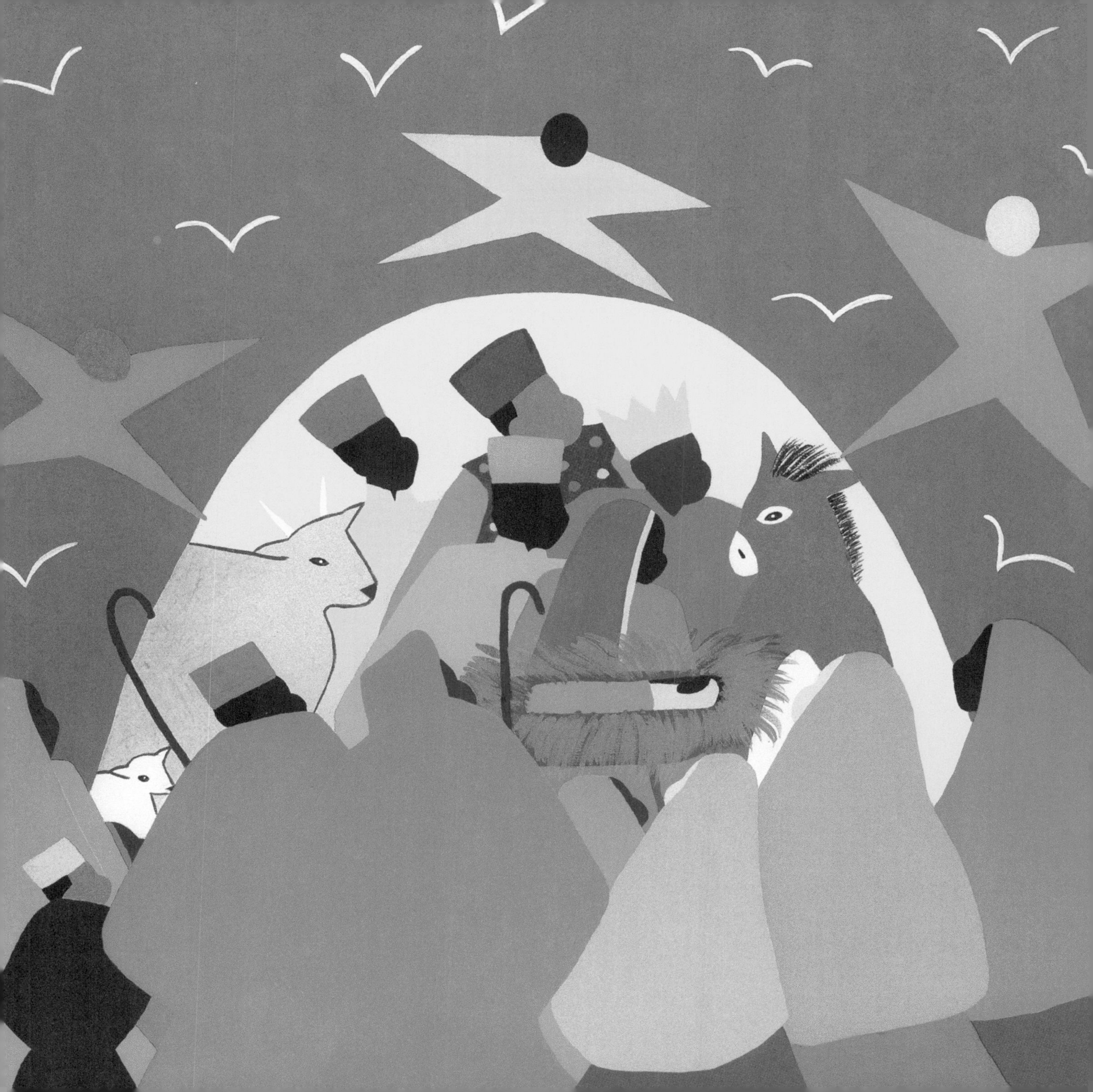

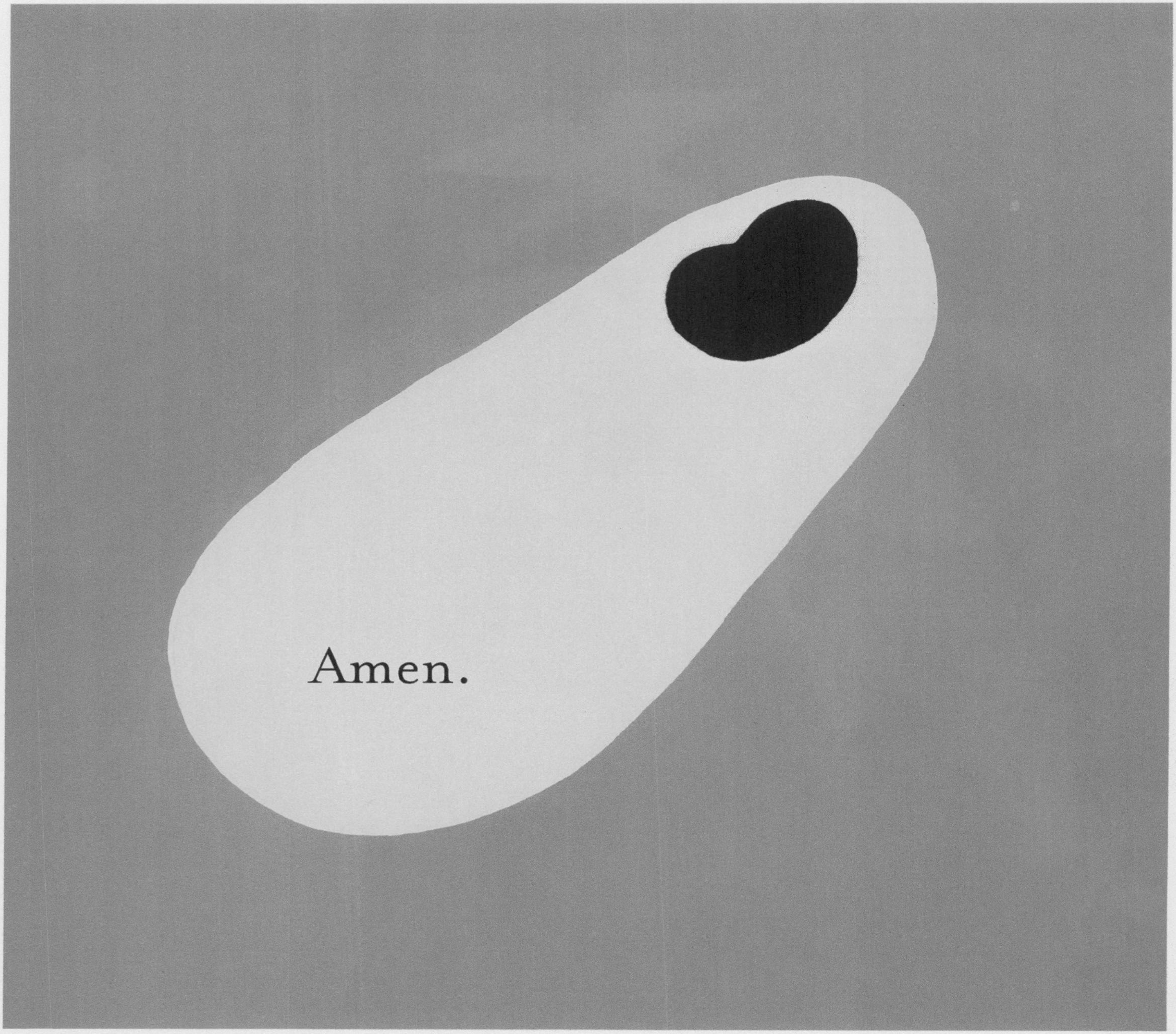
Amen.

CPSIA information can be obtained
at www.ICGtesting.com
Printed in the USA
LVHW011124181220
674466LV00002B/17